THE ELF THAT SANTA FORGOT

LADONNA NELSON KLAIS
ILLUSTRATOR SAMANTHA COBB

LifeRich Publishing is a registered trademark of The Reader's Digest Association, Inc.

LifeRich Publishing books may be ordered through booksellers or by contacting:

LifeRich Publishing
1663 Liberty Drive
Bloomington, IN 47403
www.liferichpublishing.com
1 (888) 238-8637

ISBN: 978-1-4897-0907-3 (sc)
ISBN: 978-1-4897-0906-6 (e)

Print information available on the last page.

LifeRich Publishing rev. date: 08/12/2016

One Christmas Eve Santa and his elves were busy unloading bundles of toys from Santa's sleigh on top of a sleepy farmhouse. They quietly slid them down the chimney and placed them carefully around the glistening Christmas tree.

This was the first trip with Santa for Kezia. She was the littlest elf in the group, and all the flying in the sleigh had made her very tired. None of the other elves, or Santa, noticed when she quietly curled up on the couch in the dark corner of the living room. She wanted to rest for just a moment.

But Kezia fell sound asleep. Now when Santa and the other elves left on their way to finish delivering toys all around the world, Kezia was left behind.

Kezia slept soundly until the morning sunshine began peeking through the curtains. She woke up and she stretched, looking around the room, slowly remembering where she was. Where was Santa? He was gone! Kezia was alone and very frightened.

A noise came from the hallway. Kezia darted under a rocking chair to hide just as a young boy bounded into the room.

"Mom! Dad! Come quick" he shouted at the top of his lungs. "Santa came. Look at all the stuff he brought!"

Two sleepy grownups in fuzzy bathrobes shuffled into the room and watched as the boy began tearing through the presents.

"Wow! I got the train set I wanted. I hope Santa remembered the paint set, the puppy and the toy tractors I asked for." The energetic little boy continued to throw wrapping paper all around the room as he peeled it from the packages.

"Slow down a little, Alex," his mother said, smiling. "I'm going to go fix breakfast now."

Both his mom and dad left to go get a cup of coffee, leaving Alex to finish demolishing the remaining packages.

Alex was playing with a new red racing car when the car zoomed right under the chair where Kezia was hiding. When Alex peeked underneath to look for his toy, his eyes widened with delight as he saw Kezia under there. Thinking she was a stuffed toy he had somehow missed earlier, he grabbed her by the tassle-topped hat to pull her out, pulling her hair along with it.

"Ouch! Let me go!" she demanded.

Alex jumped back, his mouth wide with surprise. "You can talk! What kind of toy are you?" he wondered aloud.

"I am not a toy at all. I am a Christmas elf" Kezia declared proudly. "I was helping Santa last night but I fell asleep and Santa left without me" she finished explaining as her lower lip began to tremble and tears trickled down her freckled cheeks.

"Don't cry." Alex comforted. "We'll get you back to the North Pole. My mom and dad will help."

"Oh, no." Kezia whispered. "Grownups can't see elves. So it must be our secret, okay?"

"Well, okay," Alex agreed. "But until Santa comes to get you, we can have lots of fun while Mom and Dad are outside doing the chores. I always have to stay in the house by myself when they milk the cows, and now I can have someone to play with."

After breakfast, when Alex's parents went outside to work, Kezia and Alex decided to call Santa on the telephone. It seemed like the best thing to do so Santa would know where Kezia was. But when Alex asked the operator for Santa's number, she was grouchy and told Alex to quit playing on the phone. Then she hung up on him!

They were not sure what to do now, so Alex and Kezia played tag in the dining room. Kezia could pop from one room to another by just waving her arms over her head. Alex was chasing after her giggling, when he knocked over his mom's potted plant. Soft brown dirt spilled all over the floor. He quickly stuffed the plant back into the pot and he got a broom and swept the dirt under a rug. But the plant looked lopsided and there was a big lump under the rug. Alex knew he was going to be in trouble now. His eyes began to fill with tears.

Kezia didn't like to see Alex sad. His brown eyes had lost their twinkle. So she blinked her eyes twice and crinkled her nose. Magically, the dirt came out from under the rug and floated back into the flowerpot by itself. Alex couldn't believe his eyes. As he watched, the plant straightened back up and looked just as it had before he knocked it over.

"How did you do that?" Alex asked amazed.

"It's easy if you are an elf" Kezia grinned. "Elves make toys, but we can also fix just about anything." She was happy that Alex was no longer sad.

The next day the two wrote a letter to Santa to tell him where Kezia was. Alex couldn't find his mom's stamps, and he had been told not to play in his daddy's desk, so he decided he would have to mail the letter without the stamp. Maybe the mailman wouldn't notice the missing stamp this one time. When Alex took the letter outside to the mailbox, he ran through melting snow and mud. Then as he ran back into the house, he left muddy footprints all over the front hall rug. When he saw the mud, he tried to clean it up himself before his mom saw what he had done. He poured a glass of water and two cups of laundry soap on the rug. That should be enough to clean it, he thought. But instead, now it was a gooey mess and looked worse than ever.

But Kezia blinked twice, crinkled her nose, and presto! The rug was clean and dry again. So were Alex's shoes. No more mud.

Alex was glad to have Kezia around to help him fix things. It seemed he was very good at making messes that he didn't mean to make. Like two days after Christmas, when he was climbing to the top of the refrigerator to get some cookies from the cookie jar.

He bumped it off the edge, and it crashed to the floor, sending broken glass and broken sugar cookies everywhere. But again, thanks to Kezia, the jar went back into one piece, and the cookies floated back into the jar before anyone else found out what had happened. And without any messy, sticky glue!

That night when everyone else was asleep, Kezia was feeling homesick. She went into the living room and sent out a HELP signal by turning the Christmas tree lights on and off, on and off, on and off. She was hoping somehow Santa would get her message and come back for her. She was having fun with Alex, but she missed her family at the North Pole.

She was about to give up when she heard a faint jingling. She tilted her pointed ears to listen carefully. The jingling came closer and closer until she heard the sleigh and the sound of muffled hoofs on the rooftop above.

A moment later Santa slipped down the chimney and hurried across the room to scoop Kezia up into his arms.

"Ho Ho little one. We've been very worried about you. I'm glad you sent that signal to show me where to find you," Santa chuckled.

Kezia was so happy to see Santa. She was anxious to go home, but she was worried about leaving Alex. She explained to Santa how lonely Alex was and how much he would miss her when she went back to the North Pole.

Santa scratched his thick white beard, deep in thought. Then his eyes lit up and he whispered a plan in Kezia's ear.

When Alex woke up the next morning, he looked under his bed for Kezia. She wasn't there. He scampered down the hall whispering her name, but he couldn't find her anywhere.

Then he spotted a single package under the bare Christmas tree. That package had not been there before. He went over and opened the lid. Out scurried a small, wriggly black puppy. She climbed up onto Alex's lap and happily licked his face.

"What's going on?" Alex's mom and dad came into the room asking. "Where did that puppy come from?" They looked at each other, very puzzled. Alex's mom found a note in the box and read …

To Alex,
This puppy needs someone to love her
and play with her.
Her name is Kezia.
Love, Santa

Alex's parents were very confused. But Alex understood perfectly. Kezia the puppy, was from his friend, Kezia the elf, so he wouldn't be lonely anymore.

Alex was happy as he could be as he hugged the puppy close.

The puppy wagged her tail excitedly as she wrinkled up her nose and began to lick Alex's face all over.